CHRISTMAS

WITH

FRIENDS

CHRISTMAS

WITH

FRIENDS

By Paula Range

Illustrated by Paula Range and
Caitlyn Pranger

Cover picture credit to:

Canva.com

ISBN-13: 9781671750586

This book is dedicated to all the kids out there. I hope you have a wonderful Christmas this year.

Thank you, Makayla for all your help getting this book out before Christmas!

CHAPTER 1

"It's beginning to look a lot like Christmas, everywhere you go!" My friends Becky, Dallas and I sang as we skipped to our lockers.

"Yippie!" My younger sixth grade sister, Grace, ran up to us in the eighth-grade hall. "Schools out! It's Christmas break!"

"Yeah!" Becky exclaimed back. "I can't wait, this will be such a fun break!"

Looking over at her I asked, "Do you have any special plans or something?"

"Oh," turning a little red faced, she added, "No, I just meant this is the first Christmas I actually have a lot of friends to hang out with over break."

Grinning Dallas responded, "Yes, me too! I'm so excited. I hope we all get together a lot over break."

So far, my school year has been rather crazy. I started my school year hanging out with the popular group. They had been my friends since kindergarten, but soon after I had fallen out of my tree house and hit my head on a rock. I began to be able to see visions of other people's lives who had been bullied. I started to see how my words and actions had been causing a lot of hurt and pain to others. But those people saw how sorry I was, and they have now become my friends. I absolutely love my new friends. This was going to be the best Christmas ever. And I had an idea I wanted to share with them all. Looking around, I decided to wait until the guys got here to tell them. Once I spotted them I couldn't stop grinning.

Waving them over, I yelled, "Hey guys, come on over. I've got something to tell you." Looking around as the bell rang, "but we've got to hurry, we have to catch the bus!"

Jonah, Tim, and Tyler walked over and stood by us. "What's up, Cat?" Jonah asked me.

"Well, I've got an idea. Since it's Christmas time, and we have so many friends this year," I looked around to see them all watching me, "what about if we draw names and do a Christmas exchange?"

"What do you mean?" Tyler asked with confusion written all over his face.

"Well, we would all put our names into a hat, then draw a name. We would then get that person a present."

"Oh! How fun!" Becky exclaimed. "Then would we have a party to exchange gifts?"

"Yeah, and have food and go sledding or something!" Grace said.

"Definitely!" I said with excitement bubbling up in me.

"Hey, I know of a cool hill we could all go sledding tomorrow, then we could draw names." Tim suggested.

"Great, where is it?" I asked.

"Just down the road from my house." Then he cleared his throat and added, "But I would rather meet at someone else's house rather than mine."

We all knew Tim's dad was an alcoholic, and he didn't want us over at his house, so I answered, "No problem, we can meet at my house and then you show us the way!"

Letting out a sigh of relief, Tim added, "Sounds good, let's meet tomorrow morning at Cat and Grace's house, and head out sledding."

"Then we can go back to our house and have hot chocolate and draw names!" Grace exclaimed as the last bell rang.

I walked off with Grace and Jonah towards our bus, "We can't forget to tell Eva once we get on the bus, I haven't seen her today." Grace said.

"Yeah, she has to come too. I'll try to sit by her on the bus and tell her." I said.

As we got on the bus, I made my way to our very new, very shy friend Eva. I couldn't stop the excitement from bursting inside of me.

This was going to be the best Christmas ever. Besides having new friends this year, I had already made out my long list of presents that I wanted for Christmas this year. Hopefully my mom found it on the fridge this morning.

This was going to be the best, lots of friends and lots of presents.

How could it get any better?

CHAPTER 2

When I woke up the next morning, I hopped right out of bed. I ran over and turned on the lights to my little Christmas tree in the corner of my room, grabbed a multi-colored candy cane, ripped it open and started sucking on it.

I glanced out my window and was so excited to see a blanket of white fluffy snow covering the ground.

I threw on many layers of warm clothes, ran out of my room and entered the kitchen. Grace was already at the table eating pancakes and bacon that my dad had cooked up.

"Hey Cat, sit down and I'll get you some breakfast in just a second."

"Okay, Dad, thanks."

Just then my mom entered the kitchen and gave a big yawn while stretching her arms.

I couldn't sit. Not with Christmas right around the corner. I jumped up and ran over to my mom.

"Did you see my Christmas list I left on the fridge?"

"Yes, I did honey, but," she then looked at me with a question in her eyes, "don't you think it's quite a long list?"

"No. Not at all. I could have added even more! The idea's kept coming to my head as I wrote them down!"

"But honey," my mom started, "It was over a page long! How can you possibly need that many gifts?"

"Need?" I asked confused. "When did Christmas *ever* become about a need? I *want* all of those presents." I whipped around and looked at my sister for help. "Right sis? Did you give mom a list?"

"Yeah, I did." She said as she took another bite of her blueberry pancakes.

"See Mom, Grace gave you a list too."

"Yes, she did, but it had five things on it."

"Five? Only five?" I looked back at my sister and she shrugged her shoulders.

"I was just going to suggest you think about it and cut some of the idea's out and hand it back to me."

To my horror my mom pulled out my list I had written out of the pocket of her robe and handed it back to me.

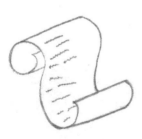

I looked and saw some of the items I had listed, the newest phone, headphones, gift cards, new boots, jeans, etc...

"Mom, how in the world am I supposed to take out any of these ideas? All the kids at school are getting these things for Christmas. I mean, that's what Christmas is all about, presents. It wouldn't be any fun without them."

She looked at me with sad eyes. "Oh, honey, Christmas is so much more than just the gifts. I hope someday you will realize that." She took a sip of her coffee and added, "Now I want you to take half of those idea's off and hand it back to me later when you're done.

"Half?"

"Yes, half."

I snatched my list out of her hand and mumbled the whole way back to the table for breakfast. My Mom had just ruined my whole day. No, she had ruined my whole Christmas.

As my friends slowly got to my house, we all bundled up in our warmest clothes. We loaded up our sleds into the back of my dad's truck.

"What's wrong?" Jonah asked me as we started to get into my mom's car.

"Nothing." I mumbled.

He looked at me like I was lying. Well, maybe I was.

"Okay, fine." I huffed. "I wrote out a list of what I *want* for Christmas and my mom said it was too long, and I have to cut it in half!"

Grinning he chuckled, "Is that it? I thought something was wrong."

"What? There *is* something wrong." I then raised my voice so my mom could hear me, "My mom is trying to ruin my Christmas."

"Oh Cat, come on." My mom said. She looked at Jonah and winked.

"What?" I looked between my mom and Jonah and asked, "Do you guys find this funny?"

"No," Jonah laughed, "not at all."

I then slouched in my seat and gave a big huff. Jonah nudged me in the arm, "Oh, come on, just forget about it for today. Let's go have fun sledding."

Easy for him to say, he was probably going to get everything he wanted for Christmas.

CHAPTER 3

As the day went on, I found I had forgotten all about my list. I was having a blast. My friends and I pulled our sleds and trudged up to the top of a very tall hill. Tim had been right, it was a great place to go sledding. We had all been taking turns riding down together. To my surprise, I had been able to stay in the sled without falling out. Grace, Dallas and Becky on the other hand had biffed it down a hill and their faces were red from the cold. But, no one wanted to stop.

"Hey Cat, do you want to ride down with me?" I heard Tim ask.

"Sure."

"Hey, guys, lets race this time. Two in a sled and we will see who can make it to the bottom first." Jonah challenged.

"You're on!" I yelled.

I looked over to my left and saw that Jonah and Eva were together, Tyler and Dallas, Becky and Grace, and Tim and me. The boys and Grace all got a running start while the rest of us sat at the front of the sleds, holding the ropes.

"Ready, set, go!" Jonah yelled.

I felt Tim jump into our sled and I pushed with all my might on the sides to get us going.

"AAAAAHHHH!" We all screamed. I didn't look behind me to see if we were ahead, I just focused on the bottom of the hill.

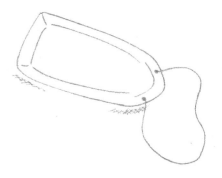

"We're going to win, Cat!" I heard Tim yell into my ear, but all of a sudden, a little kid walked right out in front of us, and we had to whip to the left to not hit him.

As we turned, we rammed into Jonah and Eva. I went flying out of the sled and my face went straight down into the cold, white, fluffy snow. Then I felt a big weight slam onto my back.

I moaned, but soon felt arms try to pull me up.

"Cat! You okay?" I could hear Tim calling my name.

I slowly pulled my face out of the snow and tried to look up at him. He was now on his knees trying to make sure I was okay. I tried to open my eyes to look at him but there was so much snow on my eye lashes, I couldn't see.

"Here," I felt Tim's fingers pull snow off my face, so I realized he had taken his gloves off. "How is that?"

Looking at him now, I answered, "Better, thanks."

"That was quite the crash, huh?"

"Yeah, and I thought we were going to win." Just then I remembered the little kid, "Hey, did we hit that little boy?"

"No, thankfully not. But, we sure scared a few years off his life."

"Years off *his* life? I think I lost ten off my own. That was freaky!"

Chuckling he asked, "Are you alright though? Do you hurt anywhere?"

"No, I'm fine."

I turned and saw Jonah helping Eva up. "Sorry guys, we didn't mean to hit you." I hollered their way.

"No big deal," Jonah said, as he helped balance a tipsy Eva. "I know you just thought we were going to win so you had to stop the race somehow." He added with a wicked grin.

"You wish! We were ahead of you. We were going to beat you, and you know it!"

"Don't waste your breath on who was *going* to win, it only matters who *really* won." Tyler walked up with Dallas grinning ear to ear.

"Beginners luck." Tim said as he grinned at Tyler. "How about we head in and warm up," looking my way he added, "Cat really took a tumble, and I think she needs some hot chocolate."

"Sounds good to me." I said. "It's almost been two hours anyways, and my parents said they would pick us up in time to have lunch."

"Food at your house always sounds good to me," Tyler said.

So, we grabbed all our sleds and started walking back towards where my parents planned to meet us.

As I crawled into the back seat of my dad's truck I realized I couldn't feel my fingers or toes as they were frozen. I really needed to warm myself up.

"Can you turn the heat on full blast, Dad?" I asked.

"Sure thing, kiddo."

I just closed my eyes and rested my head back against the seat, while I listened to my friends talk and laugh. I realized I was just going to enjoy the day with my friends, like Jonah had suggested. I would worry about my Christmas list... tomorrow.

CHAPTER 4

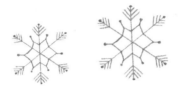

Later that same day, as we sat around the table eating chili and crackers, Becky and Grace worked on writing our names on paper and cutting them out. My dad brought in his baseball cap, and Grace threw all the names into the hat.

My dad shook the hat and held it up high. Becky was the first one to draw a name, but she got so excited and looked right at me.

"Becky! You can't do that, we all know you got Cat." Dallas said.

"Oops, sorry, I just got excited."

"Throw it back in and grab another one, just don't look at who you got."

She grabbed a different one and grinned. She then held the paper to her chest and closed her eyes. "Oh, this is so hard. I can't look at the person."

We all laughed, and my dad held out the hat to each one of us. As I grabbed my paper, I couldn't wait to see who I got. Becky. Oh, she would be so fun to buy for. I looked around and tried to read everyone's face. I wanted to try to figure out who had my name. I took my list out of my pocket and hung it on the fridge with a magnet. I hoped whoever got my name would notice my list.

"Anybody want to play a game?" Grace asked as she ran to the hallway closet. It was full of board games.

"I'd love too!" Eva said.

They all turned and ran into the living room and plopped down on the carpet. Their minds were now on the game. I sighed, so much for not worrying about my list. I looked back at the fridge and slowly walked into the living room. They might have forgotten to look at my list hanging for all to see, but I didn't forget. I couldn't forget. That piece of paper was what was going to make this the best Christmas ever.

After the games were done, I noticed the sun had started to set. The sparkling Christmas tree lights were starting to fill up the room. We all just sat back and relaxed.

"Hey guys, anyone doing anything special this Christmas?" I asked.

It stayed silent for a while. I thought no one was going to answer me so I spoke again, "I mean, I have a list of stuff I *really* want this Christmas, but my mom thinks it's too much. I told her some kids go away on these awesome trips over Christmas. We just stay here, and what is Christmas without presents?"

"Hmm," Tyler started, "I don't know about you guys, but this year is going to be very hard on me and my mom. Since my dad left us, it won't be as fun. But, my mom said she would try really hard to make it special. She said she would make an awesome breakfast. I can't wait to wake up to the smell of cinnamon rolls and bacon on Christmas morning."

"Wow, that sounds awesome. But, it's not always the most fun for me either. With my dad drinking, my mom and I kinda have to have our own Christmas together." Tim added.

"I have to say, I'm just so thankful to be alive. While I was in the hospital with cancer, I thought I was going to die. Now that I'm better, I'm just so happy to be here for Christmas." Dallas chimed in.

Boy, did I start to feel like a loser. It never crossed my mind to think of what Christmas would be like for my friends.

"But don't you want presents?" I asked.

Shrugging his shoulders, Tyler added, "Yeah, but I'd rather have my dad back."

What was wrong with me? My friends had been through a lot this year, and here I sat, mad at my mom because I didn't want to cut my long Christmas list down. All the while, my friends wouldn't have the same type of

Christmas I would have. I felt awful, like a complete idiot.

While they kept talking, I walked into the kitchen, grabbed a pencil and looked at my list. Slowly but surely, I started to erase some of the items I wanted on my list. I got rid of five items but as I erased 'a new phone', I found I couldn't take that one off. I rewrote the item on my paper and dropped my head onto the table.

"I'm a lost cause. I can't do it!" I yelled into my arms. Because as my friends laughed and enjoyed themselves in the other room, I sat in the kitchen struggling with the desire for more presents. Why couldn't anyone see that the more presents they got, the happier they would be on

Christmas morning? Was I really the *only* one who could see that?

CHAPTER 5

We decided before everyone left to get together again tomorrow. With Christmas Eve only a few days away, we needed to go shopping to get each other their gifts. Why not do it together?

The next morning came, and I was awoken when a big body slammed onto mine.

"Cat? You awake?"

I groaned, "Grace, get off me!"

"Oh, come on, you grouch." The next thing I knew, Grace had pulled my covers up and slid under them. She scooted right next to me.

"Aren't you just so excited! It's going to be so much fun today! I mean, I have Tim's name and I have no idea what in the world I will get him, but, I can't wait to go shopping together! How fun of a day this will be!"

I slid farther down under my covers. How did I tell my sister I couldn't sleep last night because I was so excited to wake up Christmas morning with all the presents under the tree?

"Hey Cat, did you hear me?"

"How could I not? You're right next to me."

"Oh, you're grumpy today." She stated.

"Sorry, I just didn't sleep much last night."

"Me neither! I'm so excited."

For some reason when my sister didn't get much sleep, it never seemed to affect her, but when I didn't get my sleep, look out world, you may not want to talk to me for the first few hours.

An hour later I found our house full of my friends. We were so excited to go shopping for the day. We were all going to pick out a gift for the person we had drawn. I also had to get something for my parents and Grace. I had been so focused on my list of what I wanted, I had forgotten to get my family something.

After we had gotten dropped off to shop, we talked about splitting up for a little bit, so people could get their person something. I went with Grace and Eva.

As we entered the first store, I reached my hand into my back pocket. I had to make sure it was still there. Not feeling anything, it felt like my heart jumped right out of my chest. Then I checked my other back pocket and relaxed. I fingered the paper. Pulling it out, I looked at my list. Even though I had scratched out some of the items, I had to bring it, just in case. In case I found something really special, that I wanted for Christmas.

The first shop we entered was full of pretty smelling candles. I took a deep breath and loved how it reminded me of Christmas. I stopped and picked up a candle that was on display. I lifted the lid and it smelled like a pine tree. Oh, I *had* to have that candle. I took out my list and grabbed the pencil I had brought, and wrote, *candle-pine scent.*

The next store had really cool shoes. I sat down and took my boots off, then I tried on a pair of name-brand tennis shoes. I stood up and walked around in them. To my surprise they were so comfortable.

"Cat, what are you doing?" My sister scowled.

"I'm just trying these cool shoes on. Do you like them?"

"Yeah, but we're shopping for Christmas gifts today. I don't want to waste time trying on shoes we aren't going to buy."

"Well, I'm going to ask for them for Christmas." I pulled out my list and pushed it in her face.

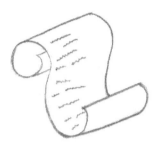

She pushed my hand away and looked at me like I was an alien or something.

"Have you looked at the price tag on those?" She asked.

"No, but I like them." I plopped down on a seat and added to my list, *athletic shoes.*

My sister just stared at me. What was wrong with her? Didn't she find anything she wanted for Christmas?

"Really, we all talked about this. Today was supposed to be fun, we're supposed to shop for other people." My sister twirled around and grabbed Eva's arm. "Come on, let's keep shopping."

"What about your sister?" Eva asked.

"She will come when she's ready. I don't want to waste our day. I have to still get my parents something."

CHAPTER 6

And that was how the next hour went. Grace and Eva had purchased gifts for both their persons and their parents, but me? I hadn't even thought about what I would get Becky. I was too busy adding to my list. When I had gotten to the stores today, my list had only ten ideas. But now that I had seen things I wanted, I had a page and a half of ideas.

Oh man, would my mom be mad at me. But how could I take anything off my list? I wanted *every single thing* on it.

I finally tucked my list away because it was almost time to meet up with everyone.

"Hey Grace."

"What?"

I could tell she was a little irritated with me.

"I kinda haven't found Becky or mom and dad anything. Do you have any ideas for me?"

I watched as she shook her head at me.

"I can't believe you. We've been to so many stores, and you haven't bought one thing."

I looked down at my feet and scuffed the toe of my shoe on the floor.

"I just need a little help." Then added, "Please."

Grace sighed, "Fine, I will help because I want Becky, mom and dad to get something nice. But really Cat, put your list away and start thinking of other people."

Ten minutes later with the help of Grace and Eva I had purchased gifts for my parents and Becky. I just wanted to get Grace something, but I couldn't with her around. I would have to find a time to slip away from her.

We ended up meeting up with the rest of the group.

Becky was grinning ear to ear.

"I just got my person a present! I think she's going to like it." She sang in a sing song voice.

"Hey! We know you've got a girl!" Tyler yelled out.

"Yeah, you said 'she'." Tim added.

"Oops," Becky's eyes got huge and she covered her mouth with her hand. "I'm so bad at this game!"

We all burst out laughing and entered the next store.

It ended up being a game machine room, so we couldn't get the guys out of there for over an hour.

After we had lunch and had bought all of our presents, we ended up in a bakery. We all grabbed a big donut and hot chocolate.

"Today has been one of the best days of my life!" Becky exclaimed.

"Yeah, it sure was fun." Dallas agreed.

"It was, but my parents are going to be here soon, so we need to take our donuts and hot chocolate with us."

So, we all stood up, grabbed napkins and balanced our cups, donuts, and presents while we walked out of the shop and stepped onto the busy sidewalk.

"I just love Christmas time. Look at all the decorations and lights filling the streets and stores!" Becky said.

"I know, and this hot chocolate really hits the spot. It's so good!" Dallas exclaimed.

"It's warming my stomach up as I drink it!" Grace added, as she took a big bite of her sugar sprinkled donut.

We all kept walking shop to shop, laughing and pointing out things we saw in the windows that we would like for Christmas.

We paused as we had to step off the sidewalk to cross what I thought was a road, but as I looked to my left I saw in between two buildings was an alley. It looked kinda spooky to me with trash bins and litter all over the ground. I started to quicken my steps, when I saw some movement down the alley.

I grabbed an arm, who's ever was closest to mine, but kept my eyes on the movement.

"What's wrong?" I heard Becky ask.

"Shh, I saw something moving over there." I pointed down the alley.

"Oh, it's probably just a cat or something."

But as I squinted my eyes, I could see the pile that I thought was trash, was not trash at all.

Becky and I both gasped as two heads popped out of the pile.

I took a step back and squeezed Becky's arm real tight.

I could barely make out the faces. They just stared at us. Then slowly, the one with longer hair started to stand up, but was pulled back down by what I could tell was an older boy.

"Cat," Becky whispered still not moving. "Did you see that little girl stand up?"

"Yeah." I tried not to move my lips, so I didn't scare them off.

"Eli! Stop pulling me down." Yelled the little girl who struggled to get out of the boy's hold.

"Emily, get down! We don't know who they are."

"But they look nice, maybe they've got food."

That's when I noticed the girl who looked to be maybe six or seven, step out of the trash pile wearing very thin sweatpants, socks with holes in them, and a too thin long-sleeved shirt. No coats, boots, hats, scarves or mittens. Absolutely nothing warm for this cold, snowy weather we were having. I could see her shivering as she crossed her arms around her tiny waist.

"Oh my gosh Becky, she's freezing!"

"Hey guys, what's taking you so long?" I heard Tyler yell out.

I turned and saw all my friends start to head back our way.

Becky and I shook our heads, my friends didn't seem to catch on. We didn't want to scare the little girl and the boy, but my friends weren't aware of what was going on.

As soon as they got to Becky and me, they looked down the alley and froze.

CHAPTER 7

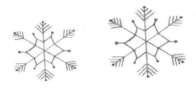

Instantly the boy who I thought was around eight or so, jumped up, pushed the little girl behind him and glared at us.

He looked no better than the girl, in his holey jeans and ripped long sleeve shirt with an old battered baseball cap. I could just make out his hair, the color of the dirt in my mom's garden sticking out from under his hat. The same color as the little girl's. But to my surprise, he stood tall, taller than me.

Now he looked as if he was close to our age.

I felt like we were in a stare down. No words were being spoken but boy were we getting some nasty glares from the boy, Eli.

I didn't want to scare them by talking. After what felt like forever, Eli spoke.

"What do you want? We don't have anything to give you, now get out of here."

"Oh," Becky's voice squeaked. "We don't want anything from you, but do *you* need anything?"

"No, we're set. Now *go!*"

But on the right side of Eli's hip popped out the little girl's face and she yelled, "F-food, do you got any f-food?"

"Shh, quiet Emily, stop talking."

"Hey man, we just want to help," Tim said. "Yeah, I've got half a donut and some hot chocolate left if you want it." Jonah replied.

Both sets of eyes looked at the food and drinks with longing.

"We don't need your help." Puffing up his very too thin chest, the older boy responded, "I can take care of my sister just fine."

"But you're both shivering. It's freezing out!" Grace exclaimed.

"I said, *we're fine.* We've got blankets."

I looked over at the pile they had been in and realized it was a shelter for them. The blankets had rips and tears all through them.

I watched as the little girl pleaded with her brother, "Please Eli, I'm so hungry and c...c...old," as her teeth chattered.

Jonah slowly took one step into the alley. Then another.

"Don't you dare come closer." Eli warned.

Jonah instantly stopped. Slowly he squatted down and laid his half donut and hot chocolate on the ground and took two steps back.

Then one by one each of us laid our left-over donuts and hot chocolate next to Jonah's.

Grace was the last to go, and as she laid her hot chocolate down, she stood and said to the boy and girl, "I'm so sorry. I ate my whole donut! Now I wish I hadn't, I'm so sorry!"

She whipped around and ran past us and around the building, but not before I saw tears streaming down her cheeks.

We all slowly backed up and walked away. With shoulders slumped, our day had just gone from fun and happy to sad and wanting to cry.

I found Grace just a few yards away. "Oh my gosh! That's so sad! And I can't believe I ate my whole donut. I didn't even need my donut, that little girl could have used it."

"Grace," Eva calmly walked over and put her arm around my sister. "It's okay, really there was plenty for them to eat between all of us."

Just then my mom and dad pulled up to the curb. "Hey kids, we were on our way to meet you, but we saw you here, are you ready to head back yet?" She looked at our packages and continued, "or do you need more time to shop?"

We all looked at each other, the joy of shopping had been smashed. "We're ready to go home now, Mom."

Half of us piled into my mom's car, while the rest piled into my dad's truck.

As we rode back I saw a worried look cross my mom's face.

She looked at me in the seat next to her, and then looked into the rearview mirror at my friends.

"Um, you okay, kids? When I dropped you off, you were so excited, and now you all look like you just lost your best friend."

When no one answered, my mom glanced my way with a question in her eyes.

I gave a big sigh and told her about the kids in the alley.

"That's so sad, kids."

"I know," I said, as I played nervously with the bags I had gotten earlier.

"Well, maybe I could call around and see if we can get some help for those two kids."

"Thanks, Mom, that would be great." I replied. But in my head, I couldn't stop thinking that Christmas was only a couple of days away. Would they get any presents for Christmas? Would they have a tree, a meal, or anything?

Or would they be huddled under that ripped up blanket alone, with nothing, absolutely nothing for Christmas?

CHAPTER 8

Two days had gone by. The days had been mixed with so many different emotions for me. I would find myself so excited for Christmas, that I had actually dreamt about the items on my list. But then, I would find myself torn, thinking of Eli and Emily, shivering in the cold, while I was tucked snuggly under warm blankets in a soft comfy bed.

As I woke up, I knew it would be a fun day. It was Christmas Eve and the gang would all come over to exchange our presents. I thought that this could be the coolest Christmas Eve in history.

I put my hand under my pillow and pulled out a copy of the list I had made for Christmas. I had no idea who had my name, but I really hoped who ever had it got something for me from off my list. But then that feeling snuck up on me again as I looked it over. It was that same feeling that had been haunting me for the past couple of days. The one tempting me to care about Emily and Eli.

But today was supposed to be fun. I had to push the sad feelings of the boy and girl in the alley aside. I needed to focus on today. So, I jumped out of bed and went into the kitchen for breakfast.

Just before my friends came, I turned the Christmas tree lights on, then started playing Christmas music softly while Grace filled the house with sugary ginger and cinnamon smells. I figured she had probably made gingerbread cookies for today.

The doorbell rang, and like always, my sister beat me to the door.

"Merry Christmas!" Grace exclaimed as she swung the door open.

One by one they entered, each holding a gift and a treat.

"Just put them under the tree!" I exclaimed.

Later, I found that the day with my friends was flying by. We had made gingerbread houses, eaten a big lunch, and decorated cookies.

"What would you kids like to do now?" My dad asked.

"Presents!" Grace exclaimed.

"Yeah!"

We all rushed into the living room with the gifts we had purchased for each other covering the floor around the tree.

"Becky, since you keep almost slipping who you have, why don't you start?" I asked. "Grab your present and give it to your person."

Becky pulled out a shiny pink present and handed it to Dallas.

Dallas unwrapped it with gusto. "Oh! I love it!" She exclaimed as she pulled out a hat that hung down long on the sides to cover her ears.

"Good!" Becky beamed. "I got it for you to help keep your head and ears warm this winter until your hair all grows out long again."

Dallas had lost her hair during her cancer treatments, but it was coming back in nicely now. It just needed time to get back to the length she had it before. That hat would work great for her.

"Thank you, Becky," Dallas said as she hugged her. "Now my turn."

Dallas grabbed the next gift and handed it to Grace. Inside was a new scarf, gloves and cookbook.

"Thanks so much!" Grace said excitedly. We watched as Grace handed Tim his gift, and he opened a new basketball. We all sat around and watched as each person opened their gifts.

It was now Jonah's turn. He walked to the tree and grabbed a large, golden box.

"Thanks," I said as I took it from Jonah's hands.

"Yup."

I slowly unwrapped the present, excitement building as I opened it. I gasped. It was a beautiful soft fuzzy blanket.

"I love it, Jonah!" Thank you so much!"

I saw his cheeks turn a darker shade of red, then he cleared his throat. "Yeah, no problem. Glad you like it."

"Like it? I love it." But as soon as I pulled it fully out of the box and snuggled it to my face, that sadness feeling came over me again.

"What's wrong? You don't like it anymore?" Jonah asked.

"Oh, no. I love it."

"Then what's wrong?"

"I don't know. It's just, as I look at all these great presents, I just can't help but think of the kids in the alley, Eli and Emily. I mean, the hat for Dallas, scarf and mittens for Grace, and this blanket would really help keep little Emily warm on these cold Michigan winter nights."

They all just stared at me. I really was not wanting to hurt Jonah's feelings. I really loved the blanket, but I had blankets in my room to keep me warm, while Emily didn't have any.

"Are you mad at me, Jonah?" I asked getting a little uncomfortable.

He gave his head a slight shake from side to side and said, "Cat, I think that's the coolest thing you've ever said."

I let out the breath I had been holding and relaxed. I was so glad I didn't hurt his feelings.

"Yeah," Tim said, "and this basketball is great," looking at Dallas. "But I already have three at home. I bet Eli would love to have one to pass the time in the alley."

"Yeah." People started to agree and chime in. We talked for a few minutes and then Grace ran into the den and grabbed tape and wrapping paper. I took off the other way to find my parents and ask them for help.

Half an hour later, we had filled the back of my dad's truck up with all the gifts we had gotten from each other. We had rewrapped them all and piled into the truck and my mom's car, ready to give them to someone who could really use them.

"Hey, can you stop at my house for just a second?" Jonah asked my dad.

"Sure," Since Jonah was my neighbor we just moved the truck a few feet.

We watched as Jonah jumped out and ran into his house.

"What's he getting kids?" My dad asked.

"I have no idea." I replied.

After a few minutes went by, we watched as Jonah came out with two winter coats and two pairs of boots.

He climbed back into the truck.

"Thanks, sir."

We all just stared at him.

"What do you have there, son?" My dad asked.

"Well, my little sister looks the same size as the little girl, Emily, and I'm about the same size as the boy, Eli. We have extra coats and boots, so I just grabbed some for them."

"Does your mom know?"

"Nope, she wasn't home, but I know my mom. She would be sending me with a lot more if she was home." He was now grinning.

My dad just nodded and looked back at the road, but not before I heard him whisper, "Nice job son, real nice."

CHAPTER 9

As we pulled up by the alley, we all started to jump out.

"Thanks, Dad." I ran up to the car in front of us and leaned in, "Thanks, Mom. We'll be right back, as soon as we give them these gifts."

"Oh no, you won't. I'm going with you. I've heard so much about them, plus," as she pulled out two plates, "I brought them hot food."

I agreed with a wide grin. I was so thankful for my mom. "Thanks, mom. Let's go."

With arms loaded with gifts, food and coats, we all walked back to the alley.

There by the pile of what I thought was trash before, stood a very tiny fire. Huddled around it, shivering, were Eli and Emily.

I heard my mom gasp. "Oh, those poor things."

I knew right when they spotted us, because Eli stood up tall, putting that protective arm around his baby sister, while Emily shrugged it off and came running.

She ran right into my legs and hugged them tight. "Thank you so, so much for the yummy donuts and hot chocolate."

As tears formed in the back of my eyes I leaned down, took my glove off to rub her little cheek. To my horror, it was freezing.

"Oh honey," I said, "you're freezing!"

"I'm-m, okay." As her teeth chattered.

"Mom!" I said whipping back around to her.

Tears were literally running down my mom's cheeks as fast and as hard as it was snowing out.

I waited as my mom looked at my dad and he gave a nod. She then looked at us and said, "Change of plans. We are not giving these kids their gifts now."

"What?" We all yelled.

"No," She shook her head.

"But Mom!" Grace and I yelled. "They need them!"

"Oh, I know girls. But we can't give them these presents and leave them here." She and my dad looked at all of us and my dad finished, "What your mom is trying to say is, we want to bring them back to our house where it is warm and let them have a place to sleep. Then they can open their presents around a real Christmas tree."

"Yah!" We all yelled.

"Wait!" Eli snapped as he walked over and pulled his sister towards him. "We don't know any of you, and you want us to just come with you?"

I watched as my mom took a few steps towards them, and spoke in a hushed tone, so only Emily and Eli could hear. If anyone could change their minds, it would be my mom. Sure enough, soon Eli nodded his head and Emily came running over to me, wrapping her little arms around me and yelled, "I get to go to your house!"

I looked over at Jonah and he handed me the shiny pink coat that had fur around the hood. I slipped Emily's arms into it and zipped it up tight.

"Let's go." I whispered.

And we all loaded our still-wrapped presents into the back of my dad's truck. Only this time we left with two extra people.

As soon as we entered the house, my mom brought Emily up to the bathroom to give her a warm bath. At the same time Eli went into our other bathroom and took a shower. While they were taking a long overdue shower and bath, Jonah rushed to his house to grab some dry clothes for them.

I stood outside the bathroom door and listened to my mom talk to Emily.

"What do you want for Christmas this year, honey?" My mom asked.

"A bunny."

"Oh my! A really bunny?"

Laughing Emily answered, "No, it would run away. I would love a soft stuffy, so I can squeeze it real tight and sleep with it."

I heard my mom mumble a reply, but I couldn't hear what she said. I slowly walked off and entered the kitchen.

I joined in and helped everyone set the table when all of a sudden, Eli walked into the room wearing Jonah's black and red flannel shirt and blue jeans. All his dirt and grime were wiped off his face and hands. His hair was combed and slicked to the side. I couldn't believe the difference. We all stood there staring, until my dad cleared his throat and clapped his hand on Eli's shoulder.

"Nice to have you in our home, find a seat and we will eat soon."

"Thank you, sir." And as he walked towards the table and passed Jonah he whispered, "Thanks for the clothes, man."

I watched as the two boys shook hands and walked over to the table together. After we sat down around the table waiting for my mom and Emily, we got to know Eli a little more. He shared how his parents had passed away about six months ago. The state said they had no choice but to separate them from each other.

"But I promised Emily that I would never let them split us up, so I ran away with her." Sitting up straighter, he added, "I have been taking care of her ever since."

Becky sat there with tears running down her face as my dad cleared his throat and took a drink of water, but not before I could see his eyes getting misty.

"See my pretty dress?"

We all turned to see a beautiful, transformed little girl twirl around in circles. She had a red Christmas dress on, with white tights, and matching bows in her hair. I jumped up from my chair and wrapped the little girl in my arms.

"You are beautiful." I told her, and whispered, "You look like an angel."

I heard a beautiful giggle come from her lips. She looked up at her brother and said, "Look at me, brother! Do I look pretty? Like mommy?"

Eli slowly scooted back and stood up. He walked over to his sister and squatted down and whispered something for his sister's ears only.

I didn't know what he told her, but whatever it was, it caused her to shake her head up and down and throw her little arms around her brother's neck and squeeze real tight. And I watched as a smile grew, which caused her whole face to look like it was actually glowing.

CHAPTER 10

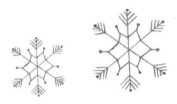

After we sat back down and ate a wonderful meal, my parents suggested that we have Eli and Emily open their gifts.

We all sat in a circle and snapped pictures with our phones, as they opened their presents from us. Eli was so excited to get a basketball, and Emily's head was covered with the hat and scarf. I could only see her eyes sticking out. An idea came to me and I grabbed one of the empty boxes and ran to my room. I had a lot of stuffed animals, and I knew I had a very soft fuzzy pink bunny. I had gotten it when I was eight. I found it under my bed and carefully stuffed it in the box.

I came back with the gift behind my back and sat by Emily. I handed her the box and she grabbed it and ripped the paper off in record time. Whipping off the top of the box, she pulled out my bunny.

"A bunny! That's what I was wanting!"

I watched as Emily hugged it and rocked it back and forth.

"This is my favorite! She's so soft and fuzzy! I love her!" She looked at me with her face all a glow, stood up and ran into my arms. "Thank you, I love her."

"Good," with a lump in my throat I added, "Take good care of her. She needs someone special to love her."

"Oh, don't worry." She looked down at my bunny and answered, "I will love her always."

"Who wants to go out and build a snowman?" Jonah asked.

"ME!" Emily yelled.

We watched as she ran to the couch and laid the bunny gently down, and then ran to the door to go outside.

"Wait! You have to dress for it." My mom yelled out and took off to get Emily dressed properly to go outside.

Once we were outside, we all ran to the back yard.

The boys wanted to make the bottom of the snowman because it was the biggest. Their goal was to make the biggest snowman they had ever seen. Grace, Dallas, Eva, and Becky rolled out the middle. That left Emily and I to make the head. We were on our hands and knees pushing the little ball when I felt a smack right on my back.

I whipped around to find the boys squatting behind the biggest snowball I had ever seen. All of a sudden Tim jumped up and threw another snow ball, this time hitting Dallas.

"Hey!" She yelled.

"Emily!" I hollered and grabbed her arm, "Hurry up, we have to get out of here!"

Off we ran to the treehouse in my yard. We tried to hide behind part of it while we frantically made snowballs.

"This is so fun!" Emily squealed.

"I know." Looking around, I told her to follow me. We ran to the side of the house and leaned against it. Trying to catch our breath, we formed a plan. Slowly taking our snowballs and pulling back our arms to aim, we jumped out and threw them with all our might. Mine smacked right into

Jonah, as Emily's fell short, which was intended for her brother.

"Hey you stinker!" Eli yelled as he took off after his sister.

She started running the other way, screaming and giggling at the same time.

I stood there smiling and watched the two of them run around. My mistake. SMACK. I looked to my right and Tim, Tyler, and Jonah were still throwing snowballs. I couldn't tell which one hit me, but I spotted the girls and ran to join them.

"The boys won't stop throwing them!" Dallas yelled.

"I know! They keep getting me." I said back.

"Anyone got a plan?" I asked.

Just then we heard Jonah yell out, "Okay guys, the fun's over, let's get back to building a snowman."

I looked at my friends and the girls just shrugged their shoulders.

"Okay, we're coming."

Our mistake. As soon as we were out in the open, the boys ran out with their arms loaded with snowballs.

"Just kidding!" Tim yelled.

"Agggh!" The girls went screaming and ducking away as the snowballs flew.

We reached the front yard and spotted Eli and Emily coming out of my house with arms loaded.

"Look what your parents gave us for the snowman!" Emily exclaimed excitedly.

They had gloves, a scarf, a carrot and much more. But sitting crooked on Emily's head was my dad's top hat.

Tim, Jonah and Tyler had joined us now, red faced and out of breath.

"You guys are jerks, you know that, right?" I mumbled, still feeling the sting from the last snowball.

"Oh, come on Cat, where's the fun in playing in the snow without a snowball fight?" Jonah smirked. I tried to give him a scowl, but I was having too much fun and I ended up with a smile on my face.

CHAPTER 11

Soon afterwards, we got three huge snowballs sitting on top of each other to form a very big snowman. It was taller than me.

Emily looked up at it while we added the final touches and said in awe, "Wow, that's the biggest snowman I've ever seen!"

Becky handed Eli the carrot and looked at Emily. He caught on and handed it to his little sister. He then gently lifted her up and she pushed the carrot right where it was supposed to go.

We all stood back and looked at what we had created. It stood tall, with a black top hat, pink and blue striped scarf, and yellow and green gloves hanging on the end of two sticks that were intended for his arms. Chocolate cookies were made for the eyes, mouth, and buttons. But long and orange was the final touch for our snowman, *the carrot.*

We all gave high-fives, just as my
mom yelled for us to come in and have
some hot chocolate. We all agreed and
headed that way.

With Emily's hand in mine, I heard her whisper to the snowman, "Bye, bye, June. I'll be back to check on you." And I watched as she waved and blew a kiss to the snowman.

"Why did you name the snowman, June?" I asked.

"It was my mommy's name. It's a pretty name, don't you think?"

I looked at her and answered, "Yes, a beautiful name. A perfect name for a snowman."

As we entered the house I was surprised to see my parent's good friends, the Shaw's, in our kitchen. They were one of my parent's best friends. They had no kids. They had wanted some so bad, but my mom said for some reason they couldn't have any. I greeted them and went to join everyone in the kitchen for some hot chocolate.

As Christmas Eve came to an end, my parents suggested we go into the living room to sing some songs before everyone had to leave. I snuck to the side and asked my mom what was going to happen to Emily and Eli.

"Well honey, they will be sleeping here tonight, but I called Mr. and Mrs. Shaw because they are certified for foster care and I know they have been wanting to adopt for years. I called them up and told them about Eli and Emily. They are very interested in taking them in and maybe if everything works out, adopt them someday."

My arms flew around my mom and I hugged her as tight as I could.

"Don't say anything tonight, honey. I have to see what the Shaw's are going to do before we say anything."

"Okay, Mom."

We then turned to walk into the living room, but I stopped and pulled on my mom's arm.

"What?" She asked.

"Thanks."

"For what?"

"Everything."

I turned and found a spot to sit and just looked around the room while everyone sang a Christmas song.

The fireplace was crackling, Christmas tree lights were shining, and the voices of many filled the room. My mom and dad sat arm in arm, while

Mr. and Mrs. Shaw sat next to Eli and Emily. Eli was on the floor with Emily, cuddled snuggly in his lap holding her bunny. My friends and sister were all sitting together, swaying and grinning as they sang.

I couldn't even sing because a lump had formed in my throat. Just a couple of days ago I had been so consumed with a Christmas list. A list full of all the things I wanted for Christmas. I had become so obsessed with it that I did not realize the gifts I already had.

I realized right then and there that this Christmas Eve was already the best Christmas I had ever had, and I had not gotten one single present. No, the gift I had was having a room full of love, laughter, friends, and family.

I jumped up and ran to my bedroom. I dug under my pillow and pulled out my Christmas list.

I ran back into the living room, walked over to the fireplace and threw my list into the fire. I watched it quickly burn. I didn't need a long list of presents to have a great Christmas. No, I had a great Christmas already. I went over and joined my friends on the floor. Becky and Grace both smiled at me and put their arms around me.

I opened my mouth and joined in, loudly singing, "*We wish you a Merry Christmas, we wish you a Merry Christmas...*"

Books by Paula Range

THE VISON SERIES

#1 - I AM "NOT" A BULLY

#2 – I AM A TREASURE SEEKER

#3 – I AM DIFFERENT

BONUS- CHRISTMAS WITH FRIENDS

I hope you have a very merry Christmas!

To find when the next book will be released please visit me on Facebook at:

www.facebook.com/paularangeauthor

Feel free to leave a review on Amazon to tell me what you think about Cat and her friends!

I love to hear from my readers. Please feel free to write me at:

paularangeauthor@gmail.com

ABOUT THE AUTHOR

Paula Range lives in the Midwest with her husband, and five children. After being a stay at home mom for 18 years, she has started her love for writing children's books. She has also been subbing and loves talking with the kids about love and kindness.

Credit to

Drawinghowtodraw.com

CPSIA information can be obtained
at www.ICGtesting.com
Printed in the USA
LVHW091341140120
643589LV00001B/105

9 781671 750586